Iain Macdo

KHUMALO'S BLANKET

Illustrated by Rhian Nest James

HODDER
Wayland

an imprint of Hodder Children's Books

One

In a small village in Africa there lived a boy called Khumalo.

His village was a happy place, with a busy market where the people traded beads, maize, fruit, goats, chickens, cattle – and blankets.

The market was famous for its blankets, and people came from great distances to buy them.

One day, Khumalo went to the market with his mother, and there he saw a beautiful blanket for sale, richly coloured with many bright woven designs.

"How much is that blanket?" he asked the weaver.

"Oh, this is a special blanket, for ceremonies and dances. I have spent many days and nights making it. But I will sell my blanket to you, Khumalo, for a large jar filled with wild forest honey," the weaver said.

Khumalo went away and thought very hard. He wanted the blanket very badly. But where could he find enough wild honey to fill a whole jar?

Then he had an idea. Calling his faithful dog, Inja, he went into the forest.

There he found a large rock and, sitting right at the top, he played some notes on his small bone flute. The notes carried far on the light breeze, and soon there was a humming of wings above him. Khumalo looked up, and over his head fluttered his friend the honeybird.

"Honeybird, I need a large jar full of honey. If you show me where I can find that much honey, I will share it with you," he said.

The bright little bird darted around him, chirping excitedly. Then it winged its way through the forest, with Khumalo and Inja running to keep up with it.

The honeybird took them straight to a huge old wild fig tree, its twisted roots sunk deep into the earth and its glossy leaves rich with small, unripe figs. A swarm of fierce African bees was buzzing around a hole in the trunk.

Khumalo covered himself with thick mud from the nearby riverbank to protect himself against stings. Then he made a pile of green branches underneath the hole and set it alight. The thick black smoke rose up and made the bees sleepy.

Khumalo climbed up the tree and put handfuls and handfuls of the delicious wild honey into a small sack.

He was so excited at finding the honey that he completely forgot to give some to the honeybird as he had promised. He ran as fast as he could back to his village, leaving the saddened honeybird and angry bees behind in the forest.

Khumalo could hardly sleep that night,
and early next morning he filled a storage
jar with the honey and went to the market.

The blanket-weaver was surprised to see
so much honey, but very glad, and he gave
Khumalo the beautiful blanket in exchange.

11

Khumalo was very proud of his new
blanket, and kept it in a special place in his
house, wearing it only when the nights were
very cold, or if there was a big dance or
ceremony in the village.

He had forgotten all about the honeybird
in the thrill of getting his blanket.

Two

Soon after Khumalo got his blanket, the
pool in the village began to dry up. This was
a very serious thing, because in Africa, water
is more precious than gold. Without water
the crops could not grow, the animals would
die and then the people would have no food.

The villagers held a big meeting to talk about what to do.

Some of them said: "Let us call in the men with the drilling machines. They will find water under the ground."

Others said: "No, we do not need the drilling machines. Someone has offended the water spirit of the Misty Mountains and he is angry with our village. We must send him gifts."

Khumalo's uncle Ngojo, the schoolteacher, wanted to call in the men with the drilling machines. But Khumalo's father, who was a farmer, believed the village should send gifts to appease the water spirit.

He and Uncle Ngojo argued about this until late into the night, while Khumalo listened drowsily, wrapped in his beautiful new blanket next to the fire.

"There is no water spirit. Those are just old stories," Uncle Ngojo said.

"Perhaps, and perhaps not. But I think that if we give the water spirit the traditional gifts of water, maize and a fine blanket, our water will return," Khumalo's father said.

Suddenly Khumalo was wide awake. What his father had said about a blanket made him remember that in his haste to get his blanket he had forgotten to give the honeybird *his* share of the honey!

Now the honeybird was angry and must have spoken to the water spirit. That was why the pool was drying up. It was all his fault!

Khumalo realized there was only one thing to do – find the honeybird and give him his share of the honey, as soon as possible.

So, early next morning, he went looking for the honeybird. But no matter where he looked, or how often he whistled on his bone flute, there was no sign of the little bird.

All day he searched until darkness fell, then, weary and sad, he returned home.

That night, Khumalo made a decision. He was to blame for the water drying up, and he was the only one who could set it right, he thought. So he decided he would go to the water spirit and give him his most precious possession – his blanket.

There and then, while everyone slept, Khumalo got up and prepared for his journey. In the morning, when the village

awoke, Khumalo had gone.

By the time the sun came up he was far away, walking through the jungle towards the plains beyond. And beyond them, towards the Misty Mountains.

In a small sack he carried some maize, and tied to his waist was a waterskin. Slung over his shoulder was his precious blanket, and by his side trotted his faithful friend, Inja.

He followed the stream that had its source high in the Misty Mountains, avoiding the deep forest where there was danger from snakes and wild animals. The stream was now a thin trickle of muddy water in a bed of sand, surrounded by dying plants and stranded fish, and Khumalo looked down at it sadly, remembering how beautiful it had been only a few days ago.

Then it had been a lively, shining ribbon of water that pushed through thick green reeds alive with brightly-coloured birds and gleaming fish. He remembered how he and his friends from the village used to splash and play in the sparkling water in the hot sunshine.

At midday, Khumalo rested in the shade of a tall Marula tree near the edge of the forest and ate a small maize cake he had brought with him. Then he moved out of the forest's comforting shade on to the hot, wide plains.

The plains were covered with long, golden grass that shone in the clear afternoon sunlight, and at their far edge rose the mighty blue walls of the Misty Mountains, their peaks sharp and hard against the sunlight.

Khumalo was careful about crossing the plains, because here there were many lions, and here the buffalo waited in tangled thickets of grass for the unwary. Here too, the elephants walked, solid and quiet as drifting grey clouds.

But this afternoon he saw none of them, and just before evening, he reached the slopes of the Misty Mountains.

He began to climb up the nearest peak, still
following the course of the dry streambed. As
the sun dropped in a fiery red ball over the
edge of the world and out of sight, Khumalo
made camp under a big overhanging rock.

Lighting a fire to stay warm and to keep any wild animals away, he sat below the big rock with Inja at his side, watching lightning beginning to dance on the skyline to the east.

Then, tired after his day's journey, he wrapped his precious blanket around himself and went to sleep.

Three

Khumalo woke up with a start in the middle
of the night to the sharp, sizzling crack of
thunder as flashes of lightning lit up the
valley below. Peering out from under the
rock, he saw the sky was full of dancing
lightning-bolts, their fiery spears crashing
into the rocks nearby.

He was frightened because he was so high up and he knew lightning was more dangerous on high ground. He crouched beneath the rock as the lightning moved closer, as if it was seeking him out with its deadly silver fingers.

Inja curled next to him, whimpering with fear, and Khumalo put his arms around him to comfort him.

 Suddenly a huge bolt of lightning hit the rock under which they crouched, flinging Khumalo some distance with the force of the blast.

He lay there, stunned, with stars whirling around and around in his head before he seemed to fall far, far down a long whirlpool into sleep.

After a long, long time he woke up to find
Inja whimpering and licking his face. Sitting
up, he felt sore all over, and dizzy.

"Stop that, Inja. I'm all right now," he
said, pushing the dog away.

But just as he
did so, Inja spun
around, his nose
pointing into the
darkness, and
began to growl.

"What is it, Inja?" Khumalo asked.
Then, from the darkness, he heard a
groan, a sound that made his eyes open wide.

"Help! Help me . . ." a voice called.

Khumalo stared into the darkness and thought he could make out a dark shape. He got up and gathered his blanket and maize, ready to run.

"Who's there?" he called out.

The shape came forward into the starlight, dragging itself wearily on its hands and knees.

Khumalo saw it was an old, old man who looked as if he had been hurt in the storm. Khumalo ran over to help him.

Seizing Khumalo's hand, the old man sat down heavily and croaked, "Water, water."

Khumalo handed over his waterskin and the old man quickly drank down every last drop.

"Who are you? What has happened?" Khumalo asked.

"I was lost in the storm. Where am I?" the old man asked. "And who are you?"

"This is the Misty Mountains. My name is Khumalo and I come from a village far away, near the forest," Khumalo told him.

"Well, Khumalo, what are you doing here?" he asked.

Khumalo did not know what to say. He thought if he told the old man why he had come to the Misty Mountains the old man would think he was foolish.

So he just said, "I was lost too."

Slowly the old man got to his feet. He was very tall and thin, wearing only a tattered piece of ancient blanket around his waist and some broken sandals held together with wire on his feet. "I'm hungry. Do you have some food?"

Khumalo nodded.

"Yes, grandfather," he said, using the polite African way of addressing an old man. "I will make you some maize porridge."

So Khumalo made a fire and cooked all the maize he had brought with him.

The old man ate it all, even licking out the bowl so there was not a drop left. Inja watched him hungrily, but the old man gave neither him nor Khumalo any.

"That is better," he said when he had finished.

"Now I am tired. Give me that warm blanket you have so I can go to sleep."

Khumalo gave him his blanket and the old man wrapped himself in its colourful folds. He soon fell fast asleep.

Khumalo sat by the fire, thinking. Now he had no maize or water to give to the water spirit. He sighed.

At least he still had his blanket. Perhaps that would make the water spirit happy.

He lay down under the rock with Inja next
to him and fell fast asleep.

The sun woke him at dawn and he sat up,
rubbing his eyes. Then suddenly he jumped
up in surprise.

The old man had gone. And he had taken
Khumalo's precious blanket!

Four

Khumalo searched everywhere, but there
was no sign of the old man.

Crossly, he turned to Inja. "Why didn't
you wake me?" he asked, but Inja just whined
softly and tried to lick Khumalo's hand.

"Now the people will have to call in the
men with the drilling machines. And we will
have to go home. We have no gifts for the
water spirit now," Khumalo said sadly.

So they started back across the golden
plains covered in shining grass, and this
time there were lions on the plains, and
buffalo too.

But Inja's sharp nose sniffed out the
animals and they went a long way around
them, without disturbing them.

Soon they were walking through the forest, Khumalo watching carefully for snakes and leopards while Inja sniffed happily at the familiar trails that led towards the village.

But when they were still some distance from the village, Khumalo suddenly stopped.

Faintly on the breeze he heard the sound of the talking drums.

The talking drums were ancient and very special, only seen by a few and entrusted to a drum-keeper. They were sacred drums made by the ancestors, handed down from generation to generation, and they were only used to send messages of great importance.

Wondering what had happened, Khumalo hurried towards the village.

At the village he found the people putting on their dancing clothes and preparing for a great feast. They were wearing swishing skirts of plaited grass and coloured cloth, with dancing-rattles around their ankles and long, bright feathers from the Sakabula bird in their hair. Everyone was shining with happiness, laughing and singing as they went about their preparations.

Khumalo ran to his father's house. "What is happening?" he asked his father.

"Where have you been?" his father asked, giving him a big hug. "We've been looking everywhere for you."

Then Khumalo told him about the honeybird, his journey to the Misty Mountains and his meeting with the old man. His father listened carefully, nodding quietly from time to time.

When he had finished, his father put his
arm around Khumalo's shoulders and said,
"Come with me."

They left the house and went down to the
village pool. When they reached it,
Khumalo stopped and stared in surprise.

The water had come back!

It gushed down the stream into the pool, overflowing the banks, bubbling up clear and clean. It splashed around the pool with a happy rush, blue and shiny and cool in the hot sunshine. It looked beautiful.

"How did this happen?" Khumalo asked.

"I think the old man you met was not really an old man, but the water spirit in disguise. By giving him your water, food and blanket you have appeased his anger towards our village," his father said.

"But why would he come in disguise?" Khumalo wondered.

"To test those who would bring him gifts. You see, there is something more than water, maize and a fine blanket that is needed to make the water spirit happy," his father added.

"What is that?" Khumalo asked.

"A kind heart. A heart that is able to give without thinking of itself."

He pointed to the clear, bubbling pool.
"Thanks to your courage and kind heart,
our village has all the water it needs. You
have passed the water spirit's test," he said.

Then he smiled.

"Your uncle Ngojo is very puzzled. In fact,
he is so puzzled that he has offered the most
beautiful blanket in the village to the person
who can tell him how the water returned.
I think we should go and see him, don't you?"

"Oh yes!" said Khumalo.

So Khumalo and his father went to see Uncle Ngojo, and after hearing Khumalo's story he presented Khumalo with a beautiful new blanket, even finer than the one Khumalo had given to the water spirit.

Then everyone danced and feasted and was very happy.

But while they feasted, Inja stayed at the pool, guarding a large chunk of honey Khumalo had left there for the honeybird.

Inja hadn't been there long when he heard the fluttering of wings above his head. And there in the sunshine was the honeybird.

Chirping happily, the bright little bird settled next to the honey and began to eat his fill.

Inja gave a soft, joyful bark of greeting, then turned away and began lapping at the clear, bubbling water of the pool. And as he did so, just for a moment, he was sure he heard someone laughing.

It sounded just like the voice of the old man from the Misty Mountains.

Look out for more enthralling titles in the Storybooks series:

Fair's Fair by Leon Garfield
It's a week before Christmas, and Jackson is frozen and starving. But the big, black dog is too, so Jackson gives it half of his pie. Little does the street urchin know what this one generous act will lead to...

Thomas and the Tinners by Jill Paton Walsh
Thomas works in the tin mine where he meets some fairy miners who cause him a great deal of trouble – but then bring good fortune. WINNER OF THE SMARTIES PRIZE.

Princess by Mistake by Penelope Lively
What would you do if, one ordinary afternoon, your sister were suddenly kidnapped by a knight and carried away to a castle? Rescue her!

The King in the Forest by Michael Morpurgo
While a boy, Tod rescues a young fawn from the King's huntsmen. Many years later, Tod finds his loyalty to his old friend the deer put to the test...

The Midnight Moropus by Joan Aiken
At midnight, on the eve of his birthday, Jon waits at the waterfall to see if the ghost of a long-dead moropus will appear...

Storybooks are available from your local bookshop or can be ordered direct from the publishers. For more information about Storybooks, write to: *The Sales Department, Macdonald Young Books, 61 Western Road, Hove, East Sussex, BN3 1JD.*